TEEN PROBLEMS

TEENS AND SEXUAL VIOLENCE

By Bethany Bryan

ReferencePoint Press®

San Diego, CA

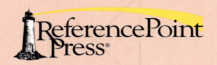

© 2021 ReferencePoint Press, Inc.
Printed in the United States

For more information, contact:
ReferencePoint Press, Inc.
PO Box 27779
San Diego, CA 92198
www.ReferencePointPress.com

ALL RIGHTS RESERVED.

No part of this work covered by the copyright hereon may be reproduced or used in any form or by any means—graphic, electronic, or mechanical, including photocopying, recording, taping, web distribution, or information storage retrieval systems—without the written permission of the publisher.

Content Consultant: Jennifer Katz, Professor of Psychology, SUNY Geneseo

---

LIBRARY OF CONGRESS CATALOGING-IN-PUBLICATION DATA

Names: Bryan, Bethany, author.
Title: Teens and sexual violence / Bethany Bryan.
Description: San Diego : ReferencePoint Press, 2020. | Series: Teen problems | Includes bibliographical references and index. | Audience: Grades 10-12
Identifiers: LCCN 2020003707 (print) | LCCN 2020003708 (eBook) | ISBN 9781682829653 (hardcover) | ISBN 9781682829660 (eBook)
Subjects: LCSH: Sexually abused teenagers--Juvenile literature. | Sex crimes--Juvenile literature. | Sex crimes--Prevention--Juvenile literature.
Classification: LCC HV6570 .B79 2020 (print) | LCC HV6570 (eBook) | DDC 364.15/30835--dc23
LC record available at https://lccn.loc.gov/2020003707
LC eBook record available at https://lccn.loc.gov/2020003708

CONTENTS

INTRODUCTION
MARY'S STORY 4

CHAPTER ONE
WHAT IS TEEN
SEXUAL VIOLENCE? 10

CHAPTER TWO
HOW DOES SEXUAL
VIOLENCE AFFECT TEENS? 32

CHAPTER THREE
HOW DOES TEEN SEXUAL
VIOLENCE AFFECT SOCIETY? 48

CHAPTER FOUR
HOW CAN WE PREVENT
TEEN SEXUAL VIOLENCE? 58

SOURCE NOTES	70
FOR FURTHER RESEARCH	74
INDEX	76
IMAGE CREDITS	79
ABOUT THE AUTHOR	80

INTRODUCTION

MARY'S STORY

In 2017 at a party in New Jersey, a sixteen-year-old boy filmed himself on his phone as he engaged in penetrative sexual acts with a sixteen-year-old girl. Both were intoxicated. Because the victim and the perpetrator were underage, court documents referred to them as "Mary" and "G.M.C.," respectively. Mary was slurring her words and stumbling when G.M.C. walked her over to a basement couch and took advantage of her sexually.

> "At the time he led Mary into the basement gym, she was visibly intoxicated and unable to walk without stumbling."[1]
> —Monmouth County prosecutor

"At the time he led Mary into the basement gym, she was visibly intoxicated and unable to walk without stumbling," wrote the case's prosecutor in court documents.[1]

According to court documents, Mary did not understand why she had bruises on her body and ripped clothing the next morning. She told her mother she was afraid that "sexual things had happened at the party."[2] After the party, G.M.C. texted

Sexual violence is a pervasive problem. Victims of sexual violence may develop depression, experience flashbacks, or develop post-traumatic stress disorder.

seven of his friends the video with the words, "When your first time having sex was rape." When Mary learned that G.M.C. was passing the video around, she asked him to stop. He refused. Mary and her family pressed charges.

In the state of New Jersey, any serious crime committed by someone over the age of fifteen can be sent to adult court. The prosecutor requested to the judge, James Troiano, that

As of 2019, all fifty states could send underage people who committed serious crimes to adult court. This allows them to be punished more severely than in juvenile court.

G.M.C. face counts of first-degree aggravated sexual assault, second-degree sexual assault, and third-degree endangering the welfare of a child, as well as two counts of third-degree invasion of privacy. The judge denied this request, saying that the "young man comes from a good family. . . . He is clearly a candidate for not just college but probably for a good college."[3]

The judge feared that trying G.M.C. in adult court would result in possible jail time and having to register as a sex offender—a designation that allows the government to keep track of offenders after they are released from jail. It also limits where the sex offender can live and work, which would likely have a devastating effect on someone's life. The judge also didn't believe that what had happened was rape. Rape, Judge Troiano said at the time of his decision, involves "generally two or more males involved, either at gunpoint or weapon, clearly manhandling a person into . . . an area where . . . there was nobody around . . . and just simply taking advantage of the person as well as beating the person, threatening the person."[4] In reality, sexual assault is defined by the US Department of Justice as "any nonconsensual act proscribed by Federal, tribal, or State law, including when the victim lacks capacity to consent."[5] Troiano thought Mary's case was only an example of a sixteen-year-old boy and girl making poor choices. In his ruling, he ignored an act of sexual violence.

Mary's story isn't an uncommon one. According to the Rape, Abuse, and Incest National Network (RAINN), an anti–sexual assault nonprofit organization, there are 433,648 victims, ages twelve and older, of rape and sexual assault each year in the United States. Teens are especially at risk of sexual violence. According to RAINN, "One in nine girls and one in fifty-three boys under the age of eighteen will experience sexual abuse or assault at the hands of

> "One in nine girls and one in fifty-three boys under the age of eighteen will experience sexual abuse or assault at the hands of an adult."[6]
>
> —*RAINN*

Sexual violence includes trying to pressure someone into unwanted sexual activity. This is called coercion.

an adult."[6] Additionally, girls from the ages of sixteen to nineteen are four times more likely than the general population to be the victims of sexual violence. Victims often struggle to get justice. Fewer than 1 percent of rapes result in a felony conviction, according to the *Washington Post*. In Mary's case, an appeals court overturned Judge Troiano's ruling and decided to try the accused as an adult. But most cases don't make it to a judge's desk at all. Victims are often afraid to report because they fear not being believed, or they fear retaliation by people who don't want the accused's life to be affected. Testifying in court often forces victims to relive the attack and have their version of events questioned.

Sexual violence is a crisis in the United States. This includes not only acts of violence and their effects on the victims, but how people talk about sexual violence. Combating all of these aspects is vital to stopping sexual violence.

CHAPTER ONE

WHAT IS TEEN SEXUAL VIOLENCE?

Sexual violence has become the focus of daily conversations on social media and in the news. But the exact definition of sexual violence can get confusing in the face of so many different accounts of violence and harassment—and with so many people attempting to blur the lines between acceptable and unacceptable behavior as they try to clear themselves of wrongdoing. What one person might consider normal and acceptable behavior might be considered problematic to someone else. So, what exactly constitutes an act of sexual violence? Sexual violence is any act in which a person experiences sexual activity without his or her consent. Consent is positively agreeing, with enthusiasm, to engage in a sex act. Sexual violence includes rape, which is defined as an act of sexual violence involving nonconsensual penetration. It also includes attempted rape, unwanted touching, pressuring

Sexual harassment includes unwanted sexual advances, verbal or physical harassment, and requests for sexual favors. Sexual violence is when sexual activity occurs without a person's consent.

someone into engaging in sexual activity, exposing one's genitals to others, or watching someone engage in private acts without his or her consent. It does not necessarily have to include physical aggression such as punching or hitting. Sexual violence can be committed by someone of the same gender or another gender, by a stranger, or by someone the victim knows, such as a relative, friend, classmate, romantic partner, or authority figure, such as a teacher or coach. More often than not, victims know

MALE ASSAULT SURVIVORS

Due to myths and attitudes surrounding sexual violence, many people believe that only women are victims. But millions of men in the United States have been victims of sexual violence. Male survivors of sexual violence may face different challenges than female survivors. Some men feel shame that they were not strong enough to fight off their attacker. These feelings are often spurred by societal views of patriarchy and masculinity. In addition, mainstream media has a tendency to treat sexual violence against men as a joke. Assault of a man by a woman is often played for laughs or treated as not a big deal in television and film. In a 2013 episode of *Glee*, a character admitted that he was molested by his babysitter when he was eleven. Two of the other boys say, "I'd kill for that," and "It's every teenage boy's fantasy." These attitudes make it hard for male victims to be taken seriously. RAINN offers resources specifically for male survivors of sexual violence. These include websites 1in6 and MaleSurvivor.org.

Glee, "Lights Out," Fox, April 25, 2013.

the perpetrator. Victims can be any age, gender, sexual orientation, or race. There's one thing that all acts of sexual violence have in common: it is never the victim's fault.

SEXUAL VIOLENCE AND TEENS

Sexual violence especially affects teens. This is partly because it is so closely tied to dating and social activities. In sexual violence cases involving children and teens, 93 percent of the victims know their attacker, according to RAINN. Date rape, or rape that is perpetrated by someone the victim knows, is a serious issue.

Since teens are generally new to dating, it can be difficult to recognize danger, especially when one is among friends and acquaintances. Misconduct, such as sexually suggestive talk or unwanted touching by an acquaintance, is often regarded as nonthreatening. Professor of criminology and sociology Heather Hlavka spoke with Slate about her research on how teenage girls talk about sexual violence. A fourteen-year-old girl talked about harassment by a male peer that she experienced every day after school. The boy told her he would "come over to her house and rape her." She told Hlavka, "I know he's joking."[7]

From an early age, girls are often told that "if a boy is mean to you, that means he likes you." This can be damaging. "It teaches kids that mean or aggressive behavior towards another person is an acceptable way to show affection," said writer Katherine on the A Mighty Girl website.[8]

Talking openly about consent and setting boundaries is important as one begins to explore sexual interactions. If someone has genuine feelings for another person, they should say and do kind things, show affection gently, and be respectful of the other person as a human being. Because every person has the right to decide what happens to his or her own body, each person

> "[Saying that a boy likes you if he's mean to you] teaches kids that mean or aggressive behavior towards another person is an acceptable way to show affection."[8]
>
> —*Katherine, writer for A Mighty Girl*

needs to consider his or her own desires and limits as well as the desires and limits of the other person.

As teens leave high school, they continue to be at risk of sexual violence. A 2014 Department of Justice report found that college women ages eighteen to twenty-four are three times more likely to be the victim of sexual violence than women of other ages, while women of the same age range who aren't in college are four times more likely than other women to be a victim. According to researchers, this may be because women who don't attend college tend to have sexual relationships at a younger age, and they may also have less supervision. The same report found that men of that age range who are in college are more likely than nonstudents to be the victim of sexual violence.

Many high school and college students who have been the victims of sexual violence on school property struggle with not being believed by school officials and not seeing those who attacked them punished fairly. In 2010, Rachel Bradshaw-Bean was raped in the band room at her high school in Texas. She reported her attack, but the school did not punish her attacker. Instead, both she and the perpetrator were sent to a school that specializes in teaching students with discipline problems. The reason was "public lewdness," or engaging in offensive behavior in a public place. "I saw him there all the time," said

SEXUAL VIOLENCE ON COLLEGE CAMPUSES

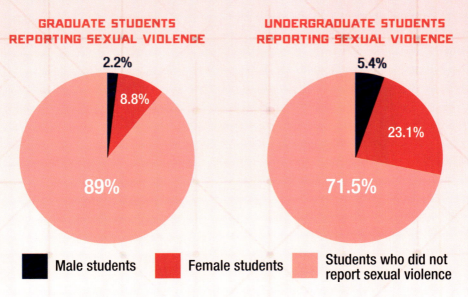

Source: "Campus Sexual Violence: Statistics," RAINN, n.d. www.rainn.org.

RAINN provides statistics on the prevalence of sexual violence on college campuses. One study asked respondents whether they had experienced sexual violence through physical force or incapacitation since entering college. The results, shown in the graphs above, found that a higher percentage of undergraduate students reported sexual violence than graduate students. Among both types of students, more women reported sexual violence than men.

Some victims struggle to get help from school officials after reporting sexual violence. This can make it difficult for victims to come forward.

Bradshaw-Bean of her attacker and her new school.[9] In 2015, a seventeen-year-old student from Missouri, Daisy Coleman, was banned from attending prom because she had accused another student of rape, and the principal couldn't guarantee she wouldn't be harassed there. A fourteen-year-old student from

Virginia was pinned down by another student who tried to take her pants off. When she saw him at school after that, she felt waves of nausea similar to what she felt during the attack. No one seemed to believe her claims. School officials later showed her a surveillance video in which she smiled a few minutes after seeing her attacker, which officials said proved she was not experiencing distress. "High schools across the country are failing to live up to their responsibility to address sexual assault and harassment," said Neena Chaudhry, an attorney with the National Women's Law Center.[10]

Colleges that receive federal funding must, under the law, report sexual assault statistics. This is because of the Clery Act, a 1990 statute that requires transparency in crime reporting. Because of this law, these schools must disclose information about crimes that occur on campus, issue warnings directly following these crimes, and create an emergency response policy to the crimes. Safeguards are different for elementary and high schools because they are affected by laws that vary state to state. Title IX, a federal rule which protects students from gender discrimination in schools, requires elementary, middle, and high school teachers or administrators to report to the police any claims of sexual violence on behalf of the student making the accusation. However, many school officials aren't trained to investigate claims of sexual violence or simply don't know what the requirements are when something like this happens. According to Break the Cycle, an organization that helps to prevent abusive relationships, 80 percent of high school guidance counselors say that they feel "ill-equipped to deal with reports of abuse on their campuses."[11] Many schools are also pushing back against Title IX, citing the cost of investigating student claims, which can be up to hundreds of thousands of dollars. Rules put in place under President Donald Trump's administration expand the rights of the accused and help protect schools from those costs, rather than protecting victims. These same rules have even changed the way some courts define sexual violence. "Some courts (though fortunately not all) have said that even a rape does not count under this standard because a one-time act of violence is not 'pervasive,'" said Dana Bolger, writing for the *New York Times*.[12]

Sometimes school officials might feel a bias toward a student who is a star athlete over the word of another student. At a college level, popular student athletes may bring in a lot of revenue for schools. Organizations like the National Collegiate Athletic Association (NCAA) often face backlash for ignoring accusations of sexual violence. University of South Florida football player LaDarrius Jackson was accused of sexual assault in 2017. The university opened an inquiry, found Jackson guilty of "non-consensual sexual intercourse," and expelled him. A year later, he started to play football for Tennessee State University. "Even when facing or convicted of criminal charges, even when suspended or expelled from school, NCAA rules allow them to transfer elsewhere and keep playing," said writer Kenny Jacoby, writing for *USA Today* in 2019.[13] These examples and many more show the lack of support to the victims of sexual violence in schools.

MARGINALIZED COMMUNITIES AND SEXUAL VIOLENCE

In 2006, activist Tarana Burke started a movement on the Myspace social network. The purpose of the movement was to reach out to survivors of sexual violence, particularly women of color and those from low-income communities, to let them know they weren't alone through one simple sentiment: Me, too. Sexual violence disproportionately affects marginalized groups of people. "The women of color, trans women, queer people—our stories get pushed aside and our pain is never prioritized," said Burke in 2019.[14]

> "The women of color, trans women, queer people—our stories get pushed aside and our pain is never prioritized."[14]
>
> —Tarana Burke, starter of #MeToo movement

More than 18 percent of African American women report being sexually assaulted during their lifetime. This number accounts only for those who report their abuse. Sexual violence goes underreported by many victims, and when it is reported, it often goes unaddressed by law enforcement and the criminal justice system.

Other vulnerable communities include immigrants, those who are disabled, and those who are LGBTQIA—lesbian, gay, bisexual, transgender, queer or questioning, intersex, and asexual or aromantic. People who are transgender do not identify with the sex they were assigned at birth. People who are cisgender do identify with the sex they were assigned at birth. A 2015 survey found that 47 percent of transgender people are sexually assaulted during their lifetime. This is partially because trans people face higher levels of poverty, stigma, and marginalization. Marginalization occurs when society mistreats a particular group because the group is viewed as insignificant. People of color who are also transgender are at an even higher risk of sexual violence. The rate is 65 percent for American Indians, 58 percent for Middle Eastern people, and 53 percent for African Americans. Many LGBTQIA people are denied help due to their sexual identity. A University of Michigan study estimates that 40 percent of women with disabilities experience sexual assault or physical violence, while more than 90 percent of all people with intellectual disabilities will be the victim of sexual assault. Research suggests perpetrators see adults with intellectual disabilities as more vulnerable because their speech may be less developed and because people may believe what they say is less credible.

WHAT CAUSES SEXUAL VIOLENCE?

There are a lot of common misconceptions about what causes sexual violence. Many blame alcohol and drug use, saying that being under the influence of a substance can cloud one's judgment. Alcohol is often a factor. At least 50 percent of student sexual assaults involve drinking, according to American Addiction Centers (AAC), a company that provides addiction treatment services. Alcohol consumption lowers one's inhibitions, making a person act with fewer restraints, and it can leave them vulnerable to being targeted, to being confused, or to failing to

CORRECTIVE RAPE

Sarah McBride, transgender advocate and national press secretary for the Human Rights Campaign, shared a story on Twitter in 2017. She had been sexually assaulted and had been hesitant to talk about her experience because she was afraid no one would believe her. Members of the LGBTQIA community are at a higher risk of sexual violence than those not part of the community. Kristen Houser is the chief public affairs officer of the National Sexual Violence Resource center. She said, "If you have a person who is expressing disdain or wanting to dehumanize another person for having a different . . . identity other than being [cisgender] or straight, sexual assault can be used as a punishment." Sexual violence intended to change an LGBTQIA person's sexual orientation is often referred to as corrective rape. This term was coined in South Africa in the early 2000s after charity workers noticed the problem becoming more prevalent. Photographer Clare Carter spent two years in South Africa speaking with victims of corrective rape. Many of the victims were assaulted by or with the help of family members.

Quoted in Alia E. Dastagir, "She Was Sexually Assaulted Within Months of Coming Out. She Isn't Alone," USA Today, *June 13, 2018. www.usatoday.com.*

Some people blame victims of sexual violence instead of the person who chose to commit the act. This is called victim-blaming.

read cues. Experts often recommend avoiding alcohol as a way of staying safe. Mike Lyttle, regional supervisor for the Tennessee Bureau of Investigation's crime lab in Nashville, called alcohol the "No. 1 date rape drug" in a 2013 *USA Today* article.[15] However, while alcohol is linked with sexual assault, it does not cause it.

Some people question how victims were dressed or ask whether they were engaging in behaviors such as dancing provocatively at a party, kissing, or flirting. This positions the accused as someone who just couldn't help themselves or misunderstood a situation, and it places the blame on the victim. In addition, victims are often blamed for drinking ("they should have been more careful"), while perpetrators are excused ("they didn't know what they were doing").

In reality, there is only one cause of sexual violence: people who choose to engage in acts of sexual violence. How victims were dressed, whether they were drinking, and how they were acting don't matter. There isn't one specific set of criteria or risk factors that leads someone down a path of committing sexual violence. However, experts believe that male sexual violence against women is the most common type of sexual violence because of a long history of misogyny. Misogyny is a bias against or contempt of women and girls.

A HISTORY OF MISOGYNY

Throughout history, women have been treated as inferior to men. The Greek philosopher Aristotle wrote that men by nature were made to be superior to women. Charles Darwin believed the same, writing in his 1871 book *The Descent of Man* that men are intellectually superior. Women were considered unable to make logical decisions. In the United States, all women were denied the right to vote until the passage of the Nineteenth Amendment in 1920. Even then, it took many more years of struggle before women of color were guaranteed the right to vote. Women weren't allowed to own property. For many women, housework and motherhood were their only career options. Many of the ones who did work for pay outside of the home were limited to teaching, nursing, or working in secretarial positions, and they were paid less than men. Moving into the twenty-first century, women gained more equality in the eyes of the law. As a result, misogyny morphed into something less concrete but equally as dangerous.

In 2005, HarperCollins published *The Game.* Written by journalist Neil Strauss, the nonfiction book showcased pick-up artist culture, the idea that men must employ certain tools of manipulation in order to not only to "pick up" women, but pressure as many of them as possible into sex. The book sold 2.5 million copies. Books like *The Game* provided their readers with a checklist of ways to get women interested. They promised that they could fix loneliness and improve confidence. But elements of pick-up culture make dating more dangerous for women. Pick-up artists are encouraged to talk women out of their resistance, even after they've said no to sexual activity. This attitude is considered by many to put women in danger and violate their autonomy, or control over their own bodies.

Male supremacy takes misogyny a step further, positioning men as the dominant gender and women as genetically

Misogynistic ideals like pick-up culture encourage men to manipulate women. This can lead to men trying to pressure women into sexual activity.

inferior and therefore required to be submissive. These types of beliefs are not just part of history. In 2017, an engineer at Google named James Damore posted a memo to a company discussion group, sharing with fellow employees that he felt that women were underrepresented at Google because they simply couldn't handle a technical position as well as a man. These mindsets have trickled down into future generations, manifesting themselves in a variety of ways. One way they have manifested is in rape culture.

RAPE CULTURE

The term *rape culture* was originally coined in the 1970s by a group of feminists, or people who believe in equal rights for everyone, regardless of gender. Rape culture now comes up frequently online and through social media. But what is rape culture? It's a set of societal standards that have allowed sexual violence to be normalized. One example of this is how often young women are put in charge of protecting themselves from possible male perpetrators. Many women in their teens and early twenties are lectured on taking responsibility for their actions by doing things such as avoiding alcohol or parties. They're told to dress conservatively and avoid any behavior that might put them at risk. People with this type of mindset believe young men have uncontrollable urges and the women around them need to be wary. This isn't limited to younger generations. Women well established in their careers are often urged to avoid traveling or staying in hotels alone while on business trips. Women are encouraged to take cabs home after a party because it's safer than walking. This part of rape culture is costly to everyone. It implies that men are inherently violent and that women are to blame for becoming their victims. It also perpetuates myths that only men are perpetrators and only women are victims.

When sexual violence does occur, many victims then struggle with being believed. Law enforcement has been

Women are often told not to engage in behaviors such as walking alone. This policing of behavior contributes to rape culture.

known to question the victim's version of events. A 2016 article in *Rolling Stone* discusses some of the ways police officers dismiss accusations of rape. The article focuses on police in Baltimore, a city that between 2006 and 2010 recorded the highest percentage of rape cases where an officer decided that no wrongdoing had occurred. This happened at a rate of 30 percent, which is five times the national average. One Baltimore officer reportedly asked a victim, "Why are you messing that guy's life up?"[16] This implies that her accusation was an attempt to disrupt the life of an innocent man, rather than an attempt to seek justice and stop him from hurting others.

Finding a police officer who will believe the victim is only the first step. The victim must then find justice through the criminal justice system, and that can also be biased against victims. According to RAINN, out of every 1,000 sexual assaults, 230 are reported to police, forty-six lead to an arrest, and nine get referred to a prosecutor. Just five result in felony convictions. Prosecutors struggle with rape cases because very often the only evidence is the word of the victim. This can make it difficult to prove beyond reasonable doubt that the defendant is guilty. Because of the unlikelihood of a conviction and because of fear of backlash, many victims choose not to press charges at all. "I think there's fear of shaming," says Soraya Chemaly of the Women's Media Center Speech Project, "of blaming, of retaliation, of being doubted. It's very hard, because we have a cultural predisposition to perpetuate a lot of rape myths. And one of those is that women excessively exaggerate as victims, that they make things up, that there are misinterpretations."[17]

> "I think there's fear of shaming, of blaming, of retaliation, of being doubted."[17]
>
> —*Soraya Chemaly on why she believes women don't report sexual assaults*

Though the bias present in the criminal justice system can be discouraging, there are systems in place to help victims. The National Sexual Assault Hotline (1-800-656-HOPE) can connect victims with local sexual assault service providers.

These centers have staff members who can help survivors through the process of getting help and reporting to law enforcement, if they so choose. Most police departments have officers specifically trained to interact with survivors of sexual assault. They may also be connected with a Sexual Assault Response Team (SART). SARTs help law enforcement, medical personnel, and sexual assault service providers work together on investigation and improve communication, prioritizing the victim. If a case does go to court, many assault cases are resolved with a plea bargain. In these cases, a survivor does not have to testify. If a survivor does have to testify, some areas allow survivors to bring an advocate, such as a trained staff member from a sexual assault service provider. Whether or not a victim chooses to report an assault to law enforcement, there are systems in place to provide support.

Rape culture is also apparent in the normalization of rape in mainstream media. Women are often objectified in movies and music. Objectification means to reduce someone to the status of an object. In 2013, Robin Thicke released a song called "Blurred Lines." The popular song sparked a controversy over lyrics such as, "You know you want it" and "I hate these blurred lines."[18] Edinburgh University Students' Association (EUSA) was the first student body to ban the song. It was followed by several others. Kirsty Haigh, EUSA's vice-president, said, "This is about ensuring that everyone is fully aware that you need enthusiastic

Shonda Rhimes (left) and Betsy Beers (right) created the hit shows *Scandal* (starring Kerry Washington [center]) and *Grey's Anatomy*. Both shows have been praised for their treatment of sexual violence.

consent before sex. The song says: 'You know you want it.' Well, you can't know they want it unless they tell you they want it."[19] In television and movies, writers often rely on tropes, or commonly used themes. In television especially, the sexual assault of women has become a problematic trope. There are examples of thoughtful and sensitive treatments of sexual violence in the media; shows such as *Grey's Anatomy*, *Scandal*, *Jessica Jones*, and *Orange Is the New Black* have all been praised on this front.

But more often than not, a sexual assault is used for shock value or to motivate a male character, and this is where it becomes problematic. A journalist with *Variety* spoke with creators on the issue for an article. FX CEO John Landgraf said, "To me, it's not so much that the very notion of sexual violence against women is taboo or shouldn't be done . . . It's that if you do it over and over and over from the context of ultimately what it means to the man, then you're just being lazy."[20] Michelle Lovretta is the executive producer and showrunner of *Lost Girl* and *Killjoys*. She said, "Sometimes going there is valid and powerful. Sometimes it's lazy and exploitative. The difference comes down to why you're telling this story, who you're telling it through, and what you're saying in the process."[21] While many content creators are working to combat the problem, this blind acceptance of rape in mainstream media continues to occur.

CHAPTER TWO

HOW DOES SEXUAL VIOLENCE AFFECT TEENS?

In late 2018, Americans kept a close watch on the confirmation hearings that determined whether Supreme Court nominee Brett Kavanaugh was suitable to sit on the highest court in the nation. Earlier that summer, a Democratic lawmaker received a confidential letter from a woman who alleged that when she was fifteen years old, she was pinned to a bed and groped by a teenage boy while they both were at a party. The boy tried to remove her clothes and covered her mouth when she tried to scream. The young woman escaped and didn't speak of the incident to anyone until years later. When she saw that her alleged attacker had been nominated to the Supreme Court, she decided to take action. The woman's name was Christine

Many Americans protested Brett Kavanaugh's nomination to the US Supreme Court. They thanked Christine Blasey Ford for coming forward with her story.

Blasey Ford, and she spoke about the attack in front of the Senate Judiciary Committee on September 27, 2018.

Even three decades after the incident, Ford, a professor at Palo Alto University, suffered from the effects of her assault. She saw a therapist as an adult to talk about the rape attempt. "I think it derailed me substantially for four or five years," she said in an interview with the *Washington Post*.[22] She believes that the incident contributed to post-traumatic stress disorder (PTSD) and anxiety that followed her into adulthood.

EFFECTS ON THE BODY

The effects of sexual violence vary for each victim. Often there are no bruises or visible signs of physical injury. But there are always effects, and even if the effects are primarily mental, emotional, or social, there may be physical effects as well.

Pregnancy is a risk when someone inserts a penis into a vagina without using a barrier method of protection, such as a condom. In some cases, such penetration occurs as part of an act of sexual violence. In a 2012 interview, Congressman Todd Akin of Missouri said, "If it's a legitimate rape, the female body has ways to try to shut that whole thing down."[23] He thought that rape doesn't lead to pregnancy because the body will prevent that from happening. This is false.

According to the Centers for Disease Control and Prevention (CDC), almost 3 million American women have experienced a pregnancy as a result of rape in their lifetime. Akin's comments were immediately criticized by his political opponents and on social media. President Barack Obama said in response, "The idea that we should be parsing and qualifying rape . . . doesn't make sense to the American people and certainly doesn't make sense to me."[24] Reproductive systems function the same whether penetration is consensual or not. When a person of

Unwanted pregnancy can be a risk after sexual violence. Victims can choose to take emergency contraception to avoid becoming pregnant.

childbearing age with a functioning female reproductive system is raped, that person may become pregnant. Pregnancy is a life-altering condition, perhaps especially for a teenager, whose education and personal life may be disrupted. Planned Parenthood, an organization that provides educational and health care services for women, recommends emergency contraception—sometimes called Plan B—within five days of a rape if the victim is concerned about pregnancy. This is an over-the-counter medication available at pharmacies, which means someone does not need a prescription to take it. There are no age restrictions for buying emergency contraception, but young people often find the purchase easier to make if they bring a friend or trusted loved one.

SEXUALLY TRANSMITTED INFECTIONS

Sexual violence also involves risk for contracting a sexually transmitted infection (STI). If a rape occurs and the victim feels safe going to the police, part of the police investigation involves a sexual assault forensic exam, often known as a rape kit. This exam allows a specially trained medical professional to treat the victim's injuries and collect evidence, such as hairs, fibers, or fluids that may contain an attacker's DNA. A medical professional will often offer preventative care or treatment for STIs at the end of an exam or ask the victim to schedule a follow-up to make sure that he or she is physically safe and healthy. Many STIs can have long-term effects, especially if left untreated. Untreated chlamydia and gonorrhea, which are generally cured with antibiotics, can lead to pelvic inflammatory disease, which can cause permanent damage to reproductive organs. Screening for incurable infections like HIV, herpes, and hepatitis is also important. If a victim of sexual violence decides against going to the police, he or she should still schedule an appointment with a doctor and get tested for STIs. Planned Parenthood health centers offer low-cost STI testing for people of all genders, as well as preventative vaccines. Planned Parenthood protects their patients' confidentiality, although their medical professionals might encourage a teenage patient to talk to their parents. Victims can also call the National Sexual Assault Hotline to be connected with a local sexual assault service provider. These providers can connect victims with health care facilities.

EFFECTS ON THE MIND

The potential physical effects of sexual violence are only part of what a victim might struggle with. Sometimes the mental and emotional effects will continue to affect a survivor even years later. Teens' brains are especially vulnerable because they are still developing. Trauma can disrupt development.

EFFECTS OF DATE RAPE DRUGS

Date rape drugs are used to make someone pass out or become impaired, making him or her unable to fight back or remember events. Common examples include gamma hydroxybutyrate (GHB), ketamine, and Rohypnol, also called roofies.

GHB slows down the function of the central nervous system, causing drowsiness. Added to a drink, GHB has no taste. GHB can slow heart rate and cause a drop in blood pressure. Ketamine lowers the heart rate and slows cognitive function. Higher doses can make a people hallucinate or feel like they're outside of their body. Rohypnol makes those who take it feel relaxed, lowering their inhibitions and causing them to black out. It can cause headaches, confusion, dizziness, nausea, and slurred speech.

Experts recommend being careful in situations involving alcohol. Don't accept drinks from anyone who can't be trusted, don't leave a drink unoccupied, and dump out any drinks that smell or taste strange. If victims suspect they may be under the effects of a date rape drug, they should ask a trusted friend for help getting to safety, call 911, or go to an emergency room.

Trauma from sexual violence can be severe. It can have lasting effects on a victim's brain development and mental health.

During a young person's teen years, their brain goes through many changes. The brain is still developing, with the help of a fatty substance called myelin. Myelin's job is to wrap itself around parts of nerve cells, essentially improving connectivity within the brain. This process is called myelination. A teenager's brain doesn't process certain things the way an adult's does.

Trauma, including the type that may be experienced during an act of sexual violence, can disrupt the process of myelination, and this disrupts brain maturation. "To cope with overwhelming experiences of distress, the brain can alter patterns of signaling from the pathways involved, which can ultimately leave those regions underdeveloped from reduced input," said writer Maia Szalavitz in *Time* magazine.[25]

One of the most profound results of trauma is PTSD. PTSD sufferers have disturbing and intense emotions and memories relating to their trauma, even long after the danger is over. They might feel sad or angry or afraid. These feelings may force them to isolate themselves or avoid anything that reminds them of the traumatic incident. In the long term, these behaviors can make it difficult for PTSD sufferers to work, go to school, and maintain connections with family and friends. Dean G. Kilpatrick is a professor with the University of South Carolina's National Violence Against Women Prevention Research Center. He notes that female rape victims are 6.2 times more likely to develop PTSD than women who have never been the victim of a sexual assault. Ninety-four percent of women who are raped experience symptoms of trauma within two weeks following the rape. For teenagers, PTSD may make them feel more impulsive or engage in risk-taking behaviors, such as binge drinking, drug abuse, dangerous driving, and risky sexual behavior.

Sexual violence can lead to anxiety and depression. Victims can lose interest in daily activities or avoid going outdoors.

Sexual violence is also linked with higher levels of anxiety and depression. A 2018 study conducted in the United Kingdom studied 137 teen girls assaulted over a two-year period. Eighty percent of the girls studied had developed a mental disorder, and 55 percent had at least two disorders. Anxiety is often perceived as simply feelings of nervousness or concern, but for many people it goes beyond that. Some feelings of anxiety are perfectly normal, such as nervousness before a test, shyness, or avoiding certain social situations. But an anxiety disorder heightens those feelings. People who suffer from clinical anxiety often experience the feeling that they are in danger. They might hyperventilate, sweat excessively, or tremble uncontrollably. Some people with anxiety might avoid going outdoors. This fear of public places is called agoraphobia. Anxiety disorders are the most common mental health issue among children and adolescents, according to the Child Mind Institute. "The adolescent brain is extraordinarily sensitive to stress," said Dr. Laurence Steinberg, who specializes in psychological development among children and teens.[26] About one in three adolescents will meet the criteria for an anxiety disorder by the time they're eighteen, and 5 percent of these cases are linked to PTSD.

> "The adolescent brain is extraordinarily sensitive to stress."[26]
> —Dr. Laurence Steinberg

Depression is also a frequent result of sexual violence. Clinical depression is a pervasive feeling of sadness that may include a loss of interest in daily activities. According to a 2017 study, women with a history of sexual assault are twice as likely to experience depression than women who have not been sexually assaulted. "Depression is one of the major after-effects of

> "Depression is one of the major after-effects of sexual harassment or assault."[27]
> —Beverly Engel, therapist

sexual harassment or assault," said therapist Beverly Engel in *Psychology Today*.[27]

Depression goes beyond feelings of sadness. People who suffer from depression often isolate themselves from others. They can feel hopeless or lose interest in the things that once brought them joy. They might feel worthless or sensitive to rejection. They might sleep too much or too little, or they may gain weight or lose weight. They might engage in self-harm behaviors such as cutting or burning themselves. They might think about suicide or even attempt to take their own life. Teens suffering from depression might struggle in school or stay home sick more often than other students. This can result in falling grades, which can be disruptive of long-term plans and goals, such as going to college or starting a career.

Self-harm is another way some survivors of sexual violence try to cope. This may include cutting, burning, pulling hair, scratching or picking at the skin, or hitting. People who do this are trying to deal with overpowering emotions, feelings of regret, and fear. Their mental anguish can be overpowering and all-encompassing. To an outside observer, self-harm might seem like a strange way to cope, but it makes sense to those who do it. Hurting oneself often offers a release or a sense of control. For someone who has survived a trauma, any sense of relief is welcome. But self-harm can cause permanent damage.

Infections are common, and an untreated infection can lead to more serious health issues such as sepsis, which is a chemical imbalance that can damage organs.

SUBSTANCE USE

Issues with substance abuse or substance use disorder may also be tied to the trauma of sexual violence. People often use drugs as a way to cope with difficult feelings, physical discomfort, or pain. Debra, who told the story of her sexual assault on the RAINN website, began using drugs to deal with suicidal thoughts and feelings of guilt and shame that were a result of sexual violence. "It made me feel like drugs were the only way out," she said.[28]

> "It made me feel like drugs were the only way out."[28]
>
> —Debra, writing for RAINN on the guilt and shame she felt after her sexual assault

Abuse of certain substances can have profound long-term effects. This is especially true for teens, whose brains are still in development. According to the US National Library of Medicine, drug use in teens can lead to long-term drug abuse when those teens become adults. Drugs can also affect a teen's physiology in the long term, weakening the immune system or damaging memory. Seeking out the help of a mental health professional is a healthier way to process the trauma caused by sexual assault.

EATING DISORDERS AND SEXUAL VIOLENCE

People who have suffered sexual trauma often find themselves dealing with an eating disorder as a result. People with eating disorders become preoccupied with thoughts, emotions, and behaviors related to eating. "Traumatic experiences, especially those involving interpersonal violence [such as sexual assault], have been found to be a significant risk factor for the development of a variety of psychiatric disorders, including eating disorders, particularly those characterized by bulimic symptoms," said Dr. Timothy Brewerton, who specializes in the link between trauma and disordered eating. People with bulimia might eat large amounts of food and then cause themselves to purge the calories, perhaps through vomiting, excessive exercise, or laxatives.

Eating disturbances happen for a number of reasons, according to RAINN. The illusion of control that comes from eating disorders may comfort survivors and make them feel in control of their lives again. Sexual violence often leaves its victims feeling powerless and looking for ways to regain some power over their own lives.

Quoted in Caitlin Hamilton, "Trauma, Sexual Assault and Eating Disorders," NEDA Blog, 2015. www.nationaleatingdisorders.org/blog.

LONG-TERM EFFECTS

Beyond effects on the body and mind of a survivor of sexual violence, there may also be long-term consequences affecting someone's ability to get a job, manage relationships, and take care of day-to-day activities.

Teenagers who are the victims of sexual violence often struggle with schoolwork and extracurricular activities following an assault. Things that once seemed important, such as getting a sports scholarship, graduating at the top of the class, or finishing a term paper, might not seem that important anymore. Victims often find their minds preoccupied, reliving their attack or going over what they could have done differently to avoid danger. "After junior year of college, I became a person who could not concentrate and was chronically absent from class," said an anonymous contributor to Inside Higher Ed, talking about her struggles with graduate school after a sexual assault in college. "I was angry, demanding and inflexible. I do not remember sleeping. I sometimes cried in closets. I lost friends. I stared out of the window during class. I struggled with substance abuse. That perfect student was gone."[29]

Victims might lash out at friends and family members, or they might withdraw from relationships altogether. Some survivors of sexual violence will also struggle to build romantic relationships, finding consensual touching or sexual activity difficult. Our Bodies Ourselves is a platform that provides information on women's health and sexuality. The initiative started with the publication of *Our Bodies, Ourselves* in the early 1970s, and the book was updated every four to seven years until 2011. The 2011 edition includes personal stories, including Gemma's. Gemma described the effect of being assaulted on her future relationships, saying, "I got into my first serious relationship senior year, after a couple of random hookups that I think I engaged in mostly to prove I was still okay with sex. I told him about it the night we were roughhousing on my bed, and he ended up on top of me. . . . I felt like I needed to explain why I looked so scared."[30]

Survivors of sexual violence might also struggle to do things that most people do without a second thought. Visiting a doctor or dentist might trigger some anxiety. A dentist in Melbourne, Australia, Sharonne Zaks, is working to train other dentists to specialize in trauma-led care, which helps to soothe patients who are recovering from sexual trauma. "For example, the horizontal chair position, they're sort of back in the same physical position as the trauma, lying under an authority figure, and that's a really strong trigger for memory," Zaks said in an interview with SBS News.[31] Rather than rushing through appointments, dentists with this type of training urge patients to bring a friend for support, play comforting music, or talk through any concerns.

Healthline and the National Sexual Violence Resource Center suggest similar coping mechanisms for more invasive doctor's appointments, such as a pelvic exam. The first step is finding a trauma-informed care physician. Healthline writer Tiffany Onyejiaka says, "Currently, the best way to find a trauma-informed care provider is by word-of-mouth referrals. . . . You can find a list of national rape crisis centers, who can act as a resource for referrals."[32] Once at the doctor, patients can talk through what to expect with their doctor and ask questions,

Some survivors can struggle with normal doctor or dentist appointments. These appointments can trigger memories of sexual violence.

bring a friend or loved one for support, or use techniques such as breathing exercises to stay grounded.

Sexual violence affects all survivors differently. There are many possible physical and mental effects and no "right" way to recover. Visiting with a mental health professional may be key to working through long-term issues as a result of sexual violence. Survivors can also reach out to hotlines or friends and family for support. They can also practice self-care. Recovery can take a long time and a lot of effort, but it can help a survivor to feel more in control again.

CHAPTER THREE

HOW DOES TEEN SEXUAL VIOLENCE AFFECT SOCIETY?

Sexual violence causes harm beyond what it inflicts on its victims. Many people feel unsafe in a society where sexual violence is common, victims struggle to be believed, and perpetrators of sexual violence are often not punished for their actions. Fear is powerful. In general, girls and women are particularly fearful. In a survey conducted by law firm Farah and Farah, it was discovered that compared to men, "women were more than twice as likely to experience fear walking or jogging in their own neighborhood at night, allowing maintenance workers inside while home alone, and taking the garbage out alone at night."[33] This kind of fear affects everyone. The feelings of

Rape culture can cause people to feel unsafe. This is particularly true at night or when they are alone.

mistrust that are pervasive in society interfere with day-to-day human interactions, the world of dating, the workplace, and more.

AN ATMOSPHERE OF FEAR

"As a 23-year-old woman of color and of small stature, I live in constant fear and paranoia," said Jessica Salinas for the *Paisano*, a student newspaper for the University of Texas. "I never consciously place myself into situations where I can be taken advantage of by people, men especially."[34]

Jessica isn't alone in these feelings. Fear is a direct result of rape culture. Even if someone has never experienced sexual violence, they often live in fear of it. "I am plagued on a daily basis by both my paranoia and vulnerability, yet I know I am one of the lucky ones. Because I *haven't* been raped," said author Shani Jay in an article on Medium.[35]

Sexual violence creates a ripple effect, or a set of consequences that continue into the future. During the Brett Kavanaugh confirmation hearings, more than 20 million people tuned in to watch both his testimony and that of Christine Blasey Ford. In the weeks that followed, health professionals saw an uptick in visits with patients. "Stories of struggle and abuse, of trauma inflicted by people with power, have permeated my sessions with patients over the past couple of weeks," said Dr. Eve Rittenberg, a primary care physician, discussing the effects that the Kavanaugh hearings had on her practice.[36] Survivors of sexual violence and those from marginalized

> "I am plagued on a daily basis by both my paranoia and vulnerability, yet I know I am one of the lucky ones. Because I *haven't* been raped."[35]
>
> —Shani Jay, Medium

> "Stories of struggle and abuse, of trauma inflicted by people with power, have permeated my sessions with patients over the past couple of weeks."[36]
>
> —Dr. Eve Rittenberg, on the effects of the Kavanaugh hearings

communities felt a sense of fear and anxiety. Many felt overwhelmed by it.

News gets around rapidly in the age of the internet and social media. Stories of sexual violence that once stayed in local newspapers or within communities are being shared online. More people are talking about these issues. Awareness is good, but it carries with it a lot more anxiety and fear. This has consequences on everyday life in the United States. "From our televisions to our political conversations, we are inundated with messages of fear," says writer Laurie Vasquez, writing for Big Think. "We feel more afraid of the world and our own neighbors now than we have in decades. But all that fear isn't good for us. In fact, according to neuroscience, fear is killing us."[37]

> "We feel more afraid of the world and our own neighbors now than we have in decades."[37]
>
> —Laurie Vasquez, Big Think

FEAR IN DATING CULTURE

Fear affects dating culture, making it harder for people to connect with potential partners. Writer Roe McDermott matched with a man on the dating app Tinder and agreed to go on a date with him. She felt uncomfortable when he suggested they try something different for their first date: "Road trip surprise. I'll pick you up, keep about four hours free. It'll be an adventure,"

SEXUAL VIOLENCE AND UNDOCUMENTED IMMIGRANTS

Undocumented immigrants are people who live in a country without official paperwork allowing them to do so. They face an additional kind of fear: being deported after reporting sexual violence to authorities. In 2016, the United States made stricter deportation laws. As a result, fewer undocumented people report crimes of sexual violence. Laura's House is an organization in California that helps domestic violence victims. In 2016, half of the seventy new cases Laura's House received each month were from undocumented people. In 2017, that number dropped drastically because people were more afraid to ask for help. "They assume that if they call a government entity it's all connected, that they will be reported to ICE and sent away. So instead they are just taking the abuse," said Olivia Rodriguez, executive director of the Los Angeles County Domestic Violence Council. ICE, or US Immigrant and Customs Enforcement, investigates cases of undocumented immigrants.

Quoted in Jennifer Medina, "Too Scared to Report Sexual Abuse. The Fear: Deportation." New York Times, April 30, 2017. www.nytimes.com.

he said.[38] Because she was uncomfortable with the idea of being in a car with a stranger, Roe suggested instead that they go for coffee, and her potential date got angry and soon unmatched her. He was no longer interested in going out. It's unclear whether or not the man was well intentioned. Still, the fear that vulnerable populations feel isn't unfounded, especially when it comes to online dating. Between 2009 and 2014, incidents of rape following an initial online meeting rose in the United Kingdom from thirty-three to 184. The less vulnerable population of heterosexual, cisgender men struggle with dating as well. Some men struggle with knowing what's okay and what isn't when it comes to intimate acts such as kissing, touching, and sex. "It's tough for me to know where the line is because it changes from woman to woman," said Geoffrey Knight in an interview with the *Chicago Tribune*.[39] Fortunately, if someone is confused about boundaries, that person can look to the definition of affirmative consent: a certain, voluntary, and mutual decision made by those who are engaging in sexual activity.

ECONOMIC FALLOUT OF SEXUAL VIOLENCE

The effects of sexual violence are also felt economically. Survivors can spend more than $120,000 in health care costs over their lifetimes to combat the physical and mental effects of an assault, according to the CDC. In the United States, many types of insurance don't cover the cost of an abortion, even if the pregnancy is the result of a rape. If victims don't have insurance, they might also have to pay for STI treatment or treatment for other physical issues. Mental health care can put a survivor at an economic disadvantage as well. A 2017 report done by Milliman, an actuarial firm, found that a visit with a therapist is "five times as likely to be out-of-network, and thus more expensive, than a primary care [doctor's] appointment."[40] Out-of-network means the health care provider doesn't have a contract with the primary care doctor, making the visit more expensive.

Sexual violence can have an effect on society. Survivors might struggle with completing their education or doing their jobs.

Over a lifetime, the total income loss resulting from sexual violence can be as great as $241,600 per victim, according to the National Alliance to End Sexual Violence. After an attack, victims often find it more difficult to complete their education, making it harder to get a well-paying job in the future. Women who have survived sexual violence are three times more likely not to finish high school. If they do find employment, victims may continue to struggle. According to a 2018 study, victims on average "lost the equivalent of $730 in short-term productivity, and there was $110 billion in lost short-term productivity across all victims' lifetimes."[41] Not only that, but victims and their families must also pay legal costs, such as hiring an attorney. Cornell University senior lecturer Liz Karns argues that financial cost should be a part of the legal discussion when it comes to sexual violence. "Once we attach a financial cost to any kind of wrong or injury we can start discussing who should pay for that," Karns said.[42]

There is also the economic burden placed on the justice system itself. The justice system is funded by the US

WHAT IS THE GRAY AREA?

In a 2007 article for *Cosmopolitan*, writer Laura Sessions Stepp brought the term *gray rape* into mainstream media. Gray rape has become a way to describe an incident of sexual violence where someone crossed a boundary, perhaps thinking that consent was implied but discovering later that it wasn't. This was sometimes considered to happen if one or both parties were drunk or under the influence of drugs.

This term is controversial, however. Many argue that no matter the circumstances, nonconsensual sex is nonconsensual sex. Others argue that people should not view rape as less severe because of rape victims' tendencies to blame themselves. For teens, in a situation where consent might not be 100 percent given, it's best to stop and check in. Drugs and alcohol can blur the lines of consent, increasing the likelihood both of victimization and of perpetration. For this reason, it's best in those circumstances to stop any intimate activity and make sure a partner gets home safely.

If their case goes to court, survivors must be able to pay legal costs. They often have to recount traumatic experiences as part of the judicial process.

government, and the cost of gathering evidence and trying cases of sexual violence adds up. It costs roughly $1,000 to $1,500 to test a rape kit, according to Vox. As of 2018, there are an estimated 25 million rape victims living in the United States.

Sexual violence does not just affect survivors. It creates a culture of fear for people of all genders, whether or not they have been directly affected by sexual violence. The economic costs are staggering. Sexual violence is a problem everyone should be working to fix, because it affects everyone.

CHAPTER FOUR

HOW CAN WE PREVENT TEEN SEXUAL VIOLENCE?

Sexual violence has long been a problem all over the world. How can people today combat something that is so pervasive? The answer isn't simple, but there is a lot that people can do to prevent and deter sexual violence. One of the first steps is easy: honoring consent.

THE IMPORTANCE OF CONSENT

One of the most important ways to combat sexual violence is to learn about consent and what honoring consent means within sexual interactions. Consent is required before any sexual activity, whether it's a one-time hookup or a long-term relationship.

Honest discussions about consent are important in any sexual partnership. These discussions can keep people from feeling pressured into sexual activities that make them uncomfortable.

In movies, on television, and in popular literature, characters get caught up in a moment. Their eyes will meet and the next scene will find them kissing passionately. But in real life, people must be careful to ensure that any intimate act is what their partner really wants. Social peer pressure might make a teen girl feel that she has to go along with what her boyfriend wants because otherwise he'll get upset or bored with her. A young man might feel pressured by friends to invite a date over when his parents aren't home because otherwise the friends might judge him or think he's a coward. It's important in moments of intimacy to push societal pressures aside and really listen to one's partner. According to RAINN, "Consent is about communication."[43] Sexual activity should be mutually agreed upon. While some worry seeking consent might seem unromantic, others help show this isn't the case. An article on Mic highlights a Tumblr post that says, "People who are like 'asking for consent ruins the moment' have no imagination."[44] The user points out that questions such as "Do you want this?" and "May I?" can augment the mood rather than make the encounter awkward. Mic asked other respondents to share how they incorporate consent into sexual interactions. One man said, "I'll often ask, 'Is this OK?' when I start . . . touching her . . . and before oral sex and sex-sex. Women seem to really, really like this system."[45] However, activists remind people that consent is not just sexy, it's mandatory. Writing for Medium, Kristen Pizzo said, "Saying consent is 'sexy' is basically saying it is an extra special touch you can add to spice up your love life . . . . It should never be admirable for a partner to ask. It's not a little

> "Consent is about communication."[43]
> —RAINN

bonus bedroom tip found in the pages of *Cosmo*. It shouldn't be a novelty. It is mandatory. Always."[46]

The phrase *no means no* has long been used as an anti-rape slogan emphasizing the importance of consent. But a more modern phrase, *yes means yes*, seeks to take the idea a step further. Consent is a clear, enthusiastic yes. It should be given without hesitation. If a partner hesitates or stays silent, it's best to stop. Flirting isn't consent, nor is dancing close, kissing, wearing revealing clothing, or having engaged in previous consensual sexual encounters. Consent should be mutually understood each and every time sexual activity happens.

Consent can also be revoked. People can change their mind, and it's important to stop if this happens. Asking permission is a way for both partners to feel safe and heard. It shows that someone can respect another person's boundaries.

Consent can be very tricky when it comes to drugs and alcohol, however. Even if a partner has agreed to sexual activity, their state of mind also comes into play. "When people are intoxicated, sexually inexperienced, in a new situation, or acting recklessly or immature, their physical

> "When people are intoxicated, sexually inexperienced, in a new situation, or acting recklessly or immature, their physical and/or mental capacity to make informed sexual decisions is impaired or limited."[47]
>
> —*Dr. Zhana Vrangalova, sex researcher and professor*

and/or mental capacity to make informed sexual decisions is impaired or limited," said Dr. Zhana Vrangalova, a sex researcher and professor.[47]

AGE OF CONSENT

Consent can be tricky when it comes to age. There are laws in place to protect teenagers from adult predators, and they vary from state to state. Even if young people say they have consented to sexual activity, if they are below the age of consent, by law they are too young to actually consent. Young men and women have found themselves in trouble after having what they believe is consensual sex with a boyfriend or girlfriend whose age falls under the age of consent in their state. It is important to be aware of consent laws when dating and engaging in sexual activity.

However, there are older individuals who purposefully seek out younger victims. The term *grooming* describes behavior that is sometimes used by adults to coerce younger people into engaging in sexual activity. This process is gradual, as the adult slowly builds trust with their victim and eventually isolates them before sexually abusing them. Even if the victim feels like they engaged in these activities willingly at the time, they have been coerced and the act constitutes sexual violence. The best course of action in any case involving an older stranger is to avoid being alone with him or her until trust is gained.

If a partner is under the influence of drugs and alcohol, it's best to wait until both parties are sober and aware before pursuing sexual activity. This erases the possibility of misunderstandings.

BEATING RAPE CULTURE

Teens can also fight back against sexual violence by fighting back against rape culture. Educating oneself on misogyny is a good first step. Reading books written by women, particularly women who are of color or who are otherwise marginalized, is important in fighting

Everyone can take steps to eliminate rape culture. Explaining the hurtful impact of offensive words or jokes is one way to stand up for survivors.

back against misogyny and other forms of prejudice implicated in sexual violence, such as homophobia or transphobia. One might also consider taking classes that focus on gender and sexuality, watching movies by women, people of color, and people who are LGBTQIA; and following more of these types of people on social media. Teens can also get involved in student organizations that advocate for the victims of sexual violence. RAINN has premade handouts, posters, and banners to use at events that raise awareness on sexual violence. SafeBAE is another organization dedicated to ending sexual assault among high school and middle school students. It is youth-led and gives teens the tools to seek justice and engage their own communities. Becoming involved in an organization may help a person understand those whose perspectives and experiences are different from one's own, which helps to build empathy.

It also helps, on a smaller scale, to stand up to anyone who makes jokes that might be considered misogynistic, racist, homophobic, or transphobic—or jokes that make light of sexual violence. Offensive jokes can have a negative effect on marginalized communities and those who have been the victims of sexual violence in the past. "According to the CDC, one in four female college students report that they've been sexually assaulted," said writer Lindy West in a 2012 article for Jezebel. "That means that if you're a comic performing to a reasonably full room, there's a pretty good chance that at least one person in the audience has been sexually assaulted. . . . So when you make a joke in that room that trivializes rape or mocks rape victims, you are *deliberately* (because now you know!) harming those people."[48]

Sometimes friends might make a joke or say something hurtful because they think everyone around them agrees. It's easier to laugh along at a joke while disagreeing internally, but speaking out might make that friend reconsider offensive jokes in the future.

Teens can also help combat sexual violence by looking out for others and themselves. Walking friends home or to their car might help them avoid danger. It's also important to learn how to take no for an answer and to urge friends to do the same. Even something as simple as being a good listener can be an invaluable trait.

HOW SOCIETY CAN CHANGE

On October 5, 2017, the *New York Times* published a story that changed how people talk about sexual violence forever. In the article, movie producer Harvey Weinstein was accused of acts of sexual violence by multiple women, including well-known actresses Rose McGowan and Ashley Judd. In the days and weeks that

PROBLEMATIC CELEBRITIES

After accusations against Harvey Weinstein in 2017, more accusations followed against other celebrities, actors, and writers. TV news anchor Matt Lauer was fired from the *Today Show* after accusations of sexual harassment and assault went public. Writer Junot Diaz was accused of forcibly kissing a woman without her consent. Actor Kevin Spacey was written out of the Netflix series *House of Cards* after actor Anthony Rapp accused him of sexual assault when Rapp was a young teen. The accusations helped to shed light on sexual misconduct in the entertainment industry.

Many people spoke out in defense of their favorite celebrities, sure that the accusations had to be wrong. Some were even in denial that anything had occurred at all. Some argued that a person's work should be judged separately from their behavior. But at what point does that behavior become too much to ignore? Some say that people can enjoy an actor or singer's content as long as they openly acknowledge their disagreement with the way the celebrity has contributed to rape culture. Others might stop engaging with a problematic celebrity's work entirely or try to educate the celebrity on social justice.

In February 2020, Harvey Weinstein (center) was found guilty of sexually assaulting two women. He was sentenced to twenty-three years in prison.

followed, a total of eighty-seven women came forward to share their own stories of inappropriate and violent behavior at the hands of Weinstein. Online, people began to talk, some sharing their own experiences of sexual violence and showing support for the victims. Others expressed disbelief that someone they've admired for a long time was capable of such violence. Actress Lindsey Lohan said in an Instagram video, "He's never harmed me or did anything to me. We've done several movies together. I think everyone needs to stop. I think it's wrong."[49]

Lohan wasn't alone in her standpoint. A lot of people, both famous and nonfamous, weighed in, expressing doubt that the allegations were true. Weinstein was a wealthy man, so people considered the alleged victims might be after his wealth. The jury and judge disagreed. In February 2020, Weinstein was convicted of third-degree rape and sexual assault against two women. He was acquitted of two counts of predatory sexual assault—a more serious charge—as the jurors could not come to an agreement. In March 2020, Weinstein was sentenced to twenty-three years in prison. The media called it a landmark case.

In 2017, in the wake of the Weinstein accusations, actress Alyssa Milano borrowed from Burke's movement. She asked people across social media to share their own experiences of sexual violence, using the hashtag #MeToo. Many people spoke up. Other famous figures, including actors, comedians, politicians, athletes, and musicians, were accused of sexual offenses. Many were fired or forced to resign from their jobs. Others apologized and some denied any wrongdoing. The movement blew up, taking over social media. Victims finally felt they had the opportunity to be heard. "I did what I did because it was the right thing to do," Judd told the *New York Times*. "I trusted that things would fall into place."[50]

Tarana Burke started the #MeToo movement in 2006 to show survivors of sexual violence that they are not alone. The movement grew in 2017 as a result of the Harvey Weinstein accusations.

One person can't fix the misconceptions, legal injustices, and victim-blaming surrounding sexual assault, but a lot of people who work together can. In an article for *Forbes*, writer Peter Himmelman said that cisgender men must learn how to speak out against sexual injustice: "It's important because repression and violence toward women in any form, deprives society of their genius, their ingenuity, and their creativity. It is important as well, because when we neglect to respect and acknowledge even the most basic humanity of women, we severely diminish our own self worth."[51]

> "When [people] neglect to respect and acknowledge even the most basic humanity of women, we severely diminish our own self worth."[51]
> —*Peter Himmelman*, Forbes

It's also society's responsibility to believe the victims of sexual violence and provide support. Only one in five victims of sexual violence reports the crime to the police. This is often because they're afraid of not being believed. "Three little words can make all the difference: 'I believe you,'" says StartbyBelieving.org, an organization that is working toward changing the way the public responds to sexual violence.[52]

> "Three little words can make all the difference: 'I believe you.'"[52]
> —*StartbyBelieving.org*

Critics of the #MeToo movement often allege that the movement has increased the number of false accusations of sexual violence. In reality, various studies have found that only 2 to 10 percent of rape accusations between 1998 and 2018 have been proven to be false. If victims feel more comfortable coming forward and pressing charges, it will encourage others to do the same. "We can shift culture if we work in unison," said Burke in 2019.[53]

SOURCE NOTES

INTRODUCTION: MARY'S STORY

1. Quoted in "Teenager Accused of Rape Deserves Leniency Because He's from a 'Good Family,' Judge Says," *New York Times*, July 3, 2019. www.nytimes.com.
2. Quoted in "Teenager Accused of Rape Deserves Leniency."
3. Quoted in "Teenager Accused of Rape Deserves Leniency."
4. Quoted in Timothy Bella, "A Judge Cited a Teen's 'Good Family' in Declining to Charge Him as an Adult for Rape. Now, He's Resigned," *Washington Post*, July 18, 2019. www.washingtonpost.com.
5. "Sexual Assault," *United States Department of Justice*, n.d. www.justice.gov.
6. "Children and Teens: Statistics," *RAINN*, 2020. www.rainn.org.

CHAPTER 1: WHAT IS TEEN SEXUAL VIOLENCE?

7. Quoted in Haley Swenson, "'That's Just One More Barrier to Coming Forward,'" *Slate*, September 27, 2018. www.slate.com.
8. Katherine, "Never Tell Her: 'He's Mean Because He Likes You,'" *A Mighty Girl*, November 6, 2019. www.amightygirl.com.
9. Quoted in Abigail Pesta, "Kicked Out of High School for 'Public Lewdness' After Reporting Rape," *NBC News*, December 23, 2013. www.nbcnews.com.
10. Quoted in Pesta, "Kicked Out of High School."
11. Quoted in Tierney Sneed, "High Schools and Middle Schools Are Failing Victims of Sexual Assault," *US News*, March 5, 2015. www.usnews.com.
12. Dana Bolger, "Betsy DeVos's New Harassment Rules Protect School, Not Students," *New York Times*, November 27, 2018. www.nytimes.com.
13. Kenny Jacoby, "NCAA Looks the Other Way as College Athletes Punished for Sex Offenses Play On," *USA Today*, December 16, 2019. www.usatoday.com.
14. Quoted in "'Our Pain Is Never Prioritized.' #MeToo Founder Tarana Burke Says We Must Listen to 'Untold' Stories of Minority Women," *Time*, April 23, 2019. www.time.com.
15. Quoted in Jessica Bliss, "Police, Experts: Alcohol Most Common in Sexual Assaults," *USA Today*, October 28, 2013. www.usatoday.com.
16. Quoted in Soraya Chemaly, "How Police Still Fail Rape Victims," *Rolling Stone*, August 16, 2016. www.rollingstone.com.
17. Quoted in "Why We Often Don't Believe Women Who Report Sexual Assault," *PBS*, June 28, 2019. www.pbs.org.
18. Quoted in "Pharrell Says He's 'Embarrassed' by Blurred Lines Lyrics," *BBC News*, October 15, 2019. www.bbc.com.

19. Quoted in Dorian Lynskey, "Blurred Lines: The Most Controversial Song of the Decade," *Guardian*, November 13, 2013. www.theguardian.com.
20. Quoted in Maureen Ryan, "The Progress and Pitfalls of Television's Treatment of Rape," *Variety*, December 6, 2016. www.variety.com.
21. Quoted in Ryan, "The Progress and Pitfalls of Television's Treatment of Rape."

CHAPTER 2: HOW DOES SEXUAL VIOLENCE AFFECT TEENS?

22. Quoted in Emma Brown, "California Professor, Writer of Confidential Brett Kavanaugh Letter, Speaks Out About Her Allegation of Sexual Assault," *Washington Post*, September 16, 2018. www.washingtonpost.com.
23. Quoted in Kate Clancy, "Here Is Some Legitimate Science on Pregnancy and Rape," *Scientific American*, August 20, 2012. www.blogs.scientificamerican.com.
24. Quoted in "Barack Obama Reacts to Todd Akin's Rape Remarks," *BBC News*, August 20, 2012. www.bbc.com.
25. Maia Szalavitz, "Sexual and Emotional Abuse Scar the Brain in Specific Ways," *Time*, June 5, 2013. www.healthland.time.com.
26. Quoted in "Anxiety and Depression in Adolescence," *Child Mind Institute*, 2020. www.childmind.org.
27. Beverly Engel, "Why Don't Victims of Sexual Harassment Come Forward Sooner?" *Psychology Today*, November 16, 2017. www.psychologytoday.com.
28. Quoted in "Debra's Story," *RAINN*, 2020. www.rainn.org.
29. "Sexual Violence and Graduate School," *Inside Higher Ed*, April 28, 2017. www.insidehighered.com.
30. Quoted in "Our Bodies, Ourselves," *Google Books*, 2011. www.books.google.com.
31. Quoted in Maani Truu, "Why This Melbourne Woman Is Training Dentists to Care for Sexual Assault Survivors," *SBS News*, May 1, 2019. www.sbs.com.au.
32. Tiffany Onyejiaka, "A Guide to Navigating Your Pelvic Exam After Sexual Assault," *Healthline*, October 9, 2018. www.healthline.com.

CHAPTER 3: HOW DOES TEEN SEXUAL VIOLENCE AFFECT SOCIETY?

33. Quoted in Kassidy Vavra, "Women Fear Everyday Life Scenarios More Than Men, Study Shows," *New York Daily News*, February 11, 2019. www.nydailynews.com.
34. Jessica Salinas, "Rape Culture: A Cycle of Fear," *Paisano*, March 28, 2017. www.paisano-online.com.
35. Shani Jay, "I Am a Woman Who Lives in Fear of Being Raped," *Medium*, August 16, 2018. www.medium.com.

SOURCE NOTES CONTINUED

36. Quoted in Maggie Fox, "Kavanaugh Hearings Triggered Painful Memories, One Doctor Finds," *NBC News*, October 11, 2018. www.nbcnews.com.

37. Laurie Vazquez, "What Fear Does to Your Brain—and How to Stop It," *Big Think*, July 31, 2016. www.bigthink.com.

38. Roe McDermott, "Why Dating Culture Needs to Acknowledge Rape Culture," *Image*, August 18, 2019. www.image.ie.

39. Quoted in Lisa Bono, "'It's Tough for Me to Know Where the Line Is:' The #MeToo Era Is Making Dating More Confusing," *Chicago Tribune*, February 15, 2018. www.chicagotribune.com.

40. Quoted in Graison Dangor, "'Mental Health Parity' Is Still an Elusive Goal in U.S. Insurance Coverage," *NPR*, June 7, 2019. www.npr.org.

41. Quoted in Clark Merrefield, "The Multi-Trillion-Dollar Cost of Sexual Violence: Research Roundup," *Journalist's Resource*, April 19, 2019. www.journalistsresource.org.

42. Quoted in Merrefield, "The Multi-Trillion-Dollar Cost of Sexual Violence: Research Roundup."

CHAPTER 4: HOW CAN WE PREVENT TEEN SEXUAL VIOLENCE?

43. "What Consent Looks Like," *RAINN*, 2020. www.rainn.org.

44. Quoted in Nicolas DiDomizio, "This Tumblr Post Perfectly Demonstrates Why Consent Is Sexy," *Mic*, July 16, 2015. www.mic.com.

45. Quoted in DiDomizio, "This Tumblr Post Perfectly Demonstrates Why Consent Is Sexy."

46. Kristen Pizzo, "The Problem with Saying Consent Is 'Sexy,'" *Medium*, April 29, 2019. www.medium.com.

47. Zhana Vrangalova, "Everything You Need to Know About Consent That You Never Learned in Sex Ed," *Teen Vogue*, April 18, 2016. www.teenvogue.com.

48. Lindy West, "How to Make a Rape Joke," *Jezebel*, July 12, 2012. www.jezebel.com.

49. Quoted in Alexia Fernandez, "Lindsay Lohan Comes to Harvey Weinstein's Defense, 'I Feel Very Bad for Him Right Now,'" *People*, October 11, 2017. www.people.com.

50. Quoted in Jodi Kantor, "How Saying #MeToo Changed Their Lives," *New York Times*, 2020. www.nytimes.com.

51. Peter Himmelman, "How Can I Help? (Stemming the Tide of Sexual Abuse and Injustice Against Women)," *Forbes*, December 7, 2017. www.forbes.com.

52. "Start by Believing," *Start by Believing*, n.d. www.startbybelieving.org.
53. Quoted in "'Our Pain Is Never Prioritized.' #MeToo Founder Tarana Burke Says We Must Listen to 'Untold' Stories of Minority Women."

FOR FURTHER RESEARCH

BOOKS

A.W. Buckey, *Sexual Violence*. San Diego, CA: ReferencePoint Press, 2020.

Kirby Dick and Amy Ziering, *The Hunting Ground: The Inside Story of Sexual Assault on American College Campuses*. New York: Hot Books, 2016.

M.M. Eboch, ed., *The #MeToo Movement*. New York: Greenhaven Publishing, 2020.

Sherri Mabry Gordon, *Violence Against Women*. San Diego, CA: ReferencePoint Press, 2019.

Peggy J. Parks, *The #MeToo Movement*. San Diego, CA: ReferencePoint Press, 2020.

INTERNET SOURCES

Michael Dolce, "College Is Starting Again, and with It the Threat of Campus Sexual Assault. A Lawyer Offers Advice," *NBC News*, September 2, 2019. www.nbcnews.com.

Constance Grady, "The Complicated, Inadequate Language of Sexual Violence," *Vox*, November 30, 2017. www.vox.com.

Mia Mercado, "11 Organizations to Support During Sexual Assault Awareness Month & Beyond," *Bustle*, April 13, 2017. www.bustle.com.

WEBSITES

Human Rights Campaign
www.hrc.org/resources/sexual-assault-and-the-lgbt-community

The Human Rights Campaign provides resources and information, including places to go for help, to those in the LGBTQIA community.

National Sexual Violence Research Center (NSVRC)
www.nsvrc.org

The NSVRC provides information on how to prevent sexual violence and works with the media to promote accurate reporting.

RAINN
www.rainn.org

RAINN offers statistics, the latest news, and information on public policy surrounding sexual violence.

INDEX

Akin, Todd, 34
American Addiction Centers (AAC), 21
appeals court, 8–9

Big Think, 51
Blasey Ford, Christine, 32–33, 50
"Blurred Lines," 29–30
Bolger, Dana, 18
Bradshaw-Bean, Rachel, 14–16
brain development, 37–39, 41, 43
Break the Cycle, 18
Burke, Tarana, 19, 67–69

Carter, Clare, 21
Centers for Disease Control and Prevention (CDC), 34, 53, 64
Chaudhry, Neena, 17
Chemaly, Soraya, 28
Chicago Tribune, 53
Child Mind Institute, 41
Clery Act, 17
Coleman, Daisy, 16
consent, 7, 10–11, 13–14, 30, 53, 55, 58–62, 65
Cornell University, 55
corrective rape, 21
Cosmopolitan, 55, 61
court documents, 4–5

Damore, James, 25
date rape, 12, 24
date rape drugs, 22, 37
dating culture, 12, 24, 49, 51–53, 60, 62
domestic violence, 52

Edinburgh University Students' Association, 29–30
effects of sexual violence, 9, 33–47, 50, 53–56, 64
   anxiety, 34, 40–41, 46, 51
   depression, 40–42
   eating disorders, 44
   post-traumatic stress disorder (PTSD), 34, 39, 41
   pregnancy, 34–35, 53
   self-harm, 42
   sexually transmitted infections (STIs), 36
   substance abuse, 21, 39, 43, 45
   suicide, 42–43
Engel, Beverly, 41–42

fear, 9, 28, 41–42, 48–52, 57
feminists, 26

Game, The, 24
Glee, 12

Haigh, Kirsty, 29–30
HarperCollins, 24
health insurance, 53
Healthline, 46
Hlavka, Heather, 13
Houser, Kristen, 21
Human Rights Campaign, 21

immigrants, 20, 52
Inside Higher Ed, 45

Jackson, LaDarrius, 18
Jacoby, Kenny, 19
Jay, Shani, 50
Jezebel, 64

Karns, Liz, 55
Kavanaugh, Brett, 32–34, 50
Kilpatrick, Dean G., 39
Knight, Geoffrey, 53

Landgraf, John, 31
Laura's House, 52
Lovretta, Michelle, 31
Lyttle, Mike, 22

marginalized communities, 19–20, 50–51, 62–64
McBride, Sarah, 21
McDermott, Roe, 51–52
Medium, 50, 60
#MeToo, 19, 67–69
Mighty Girl, A, 13
Milliman, 53
misogyny, 23–25, 62–64
Missouri, 16, 34

National Alliance to End Sexual Violence, 54
National Collegiate Athletic Association (NCAA), 18–19
National Sexual Assault Hotline, 28, 37
National Sexual Violence Resource Center, 21, 46
National Women's Law Center, 17
New York Times, 18, 65, 67
Nineteenth Amendment, 23

Obama, Barack, 34
Onyejiaka, Tiffany, 46
Our Bodies Ourselves, 45

Paisano, 49
Palo Alto University, 33
peer pressure, 59
Pizzo, Kristen, 60
Planned Parenthood, 35–36
police, 17, 26–29, 36, 69
Psychology Today, 42

rape, 5, 7–8, 10, 12–18, 27–28, 31, 33–36, 39, 50, 52–53, 55, 56, 64, 67, 69
Rape, Abuse, and Incest National Network (RAINN), 7, 12, 15, 28, 43, 44, 60, 63
rape culture, 25–26, 29, 50, 62–65
Rapp, Anthony, 65
reporting sexual violence, 9, 14–19, 28–29, 52, 69
Rittenberg, Eve, 50
Rodriguez, Olivia, 52
Rolling Stone, 27

Salinas, Jessica, 49
SBS News, 46
Sessions Stepp, Laura, 55
sex offender, 6–7
Sexual Assault Response Team (SART), 29
sexual violence in the media, 10, 12, 29–31, 51, 55
Slate, 13
Spacey, Kevin, 65
Steinberg, Laurence, 41
Strauss, Neil, 24
Supreme Court, 32–33
Szalavitz, Maia, 39

INDEX CONTINUED

Tennessee State University, 18
Texas, 14, 49
therapy, 33, 42, 53
Thicke, Robin, 29
Time, 39
Tinder, 51
Title IX, 17–18
trauma, 37–39, 42–43, 44, 46, 50
Trump, Donald, 18

United Kingdom, 40, 52
University of South Carolina's National Violence Against Women Prevention Research Center, 39
University of South Florida, 18
University of Texas, 49
US Department of Justice, 7, 14
US National Library of Medicine, 43
USA Today, 19, 21, 22

Variety, 31
Vasquez, Laurie, 51
victim-blaming, 22–23, 26, 28, 55, 68
Virginia, 17
Vox, 56
Vrangalova, Zhana, 61–62

Washington Post, 8, 33
Weinstein, Harvey, 65–67
West, Lindy, 64
Women's Media Center Speech Project, 28

Zaks, Sharonne, 46

IMAGE CREDITS

Cover: © Hugo Felix/Shutterstock Images
5: © Kamira/Shutterstock Images
6: © Kayasit Sonsupap/Shutterstock Images
8: © bluedog studio/Shutterstock Images
11: © Yakobchuk Viacheslav/Shutterstock Images
15: © Red Line Editorial
16: © fizkes/Shutterstock Images
22: © Motortion Films/Shutterstock Images
25: © stock-eye/iStockphoto
27: © Photographee.eu/Shutterstock Images
30: © Dfree/Shutterstock Images
33: © Sundry Photography/Shutterstock Images
35: © Andriy R/Shutterstock Images
38: © pixelheadphoto digitalskillet/Shutterstock Images
40: © Monkey Business Images/Shuttestock Images
47: © Motortion Films/Shutterstock Images
49: © Mark Agnor/Shutterstock Images
54: © Mivolchan19/Shutterstock Images
56: © andresr/iStockphoto
59: © Petrenko Andriy/Shutterstock Images
63: © Iryna Inshyna/Shutterstock Images
66: © lev radin/Shutterstock Images
68: © Sundry Photography/Shutterstock Images

ABOUT THE AUTHOR

Bethany Bryan is the author of a number of books that provide guidance to teens, although she knows that readers know a lot more about certain things than she does. Sometimes she edits graphic novels. Bethany enjoys books and video games, collecting records, and advocating for quality mental health care. She lives in Kansas City, Missouri. #MeToo